The Lord's Prayer

Padre Nuestro

A Prayer Book for Children

Matthew 6:9-13
KJV

Illustrated and designed by:
Frances Palm Edwards
Mary Palm Hamilton

In English
And
In Spanish

Halo ●●●●
Publishing International

ISBN 13: 978-1-61244-120-7
Library of Congress Control Number: 2012921996

Printed in the United States of America

Halo
Publishing International
www.halopublishing.com

Published by Halo Publishing International
AP·726
P.O. Box 60326
Houston, Texas 77205
Toll Free 1-877-705-9647
www.halopublishing.com
www.holapublishing.com
e-mail: contact@halopublishing.com

This book is dedicated to our
Lord and Saviour Jesus Christ.

-Frances and Mary

Our Father, who art in heaven,

Padre nuestro, que estás en el cielo,

hallowed be thy Name;

santificado sea tu Nombre;

thy kingdom come;

venga a nosotros tu reino;

thy will be done

hágase tu voluntad

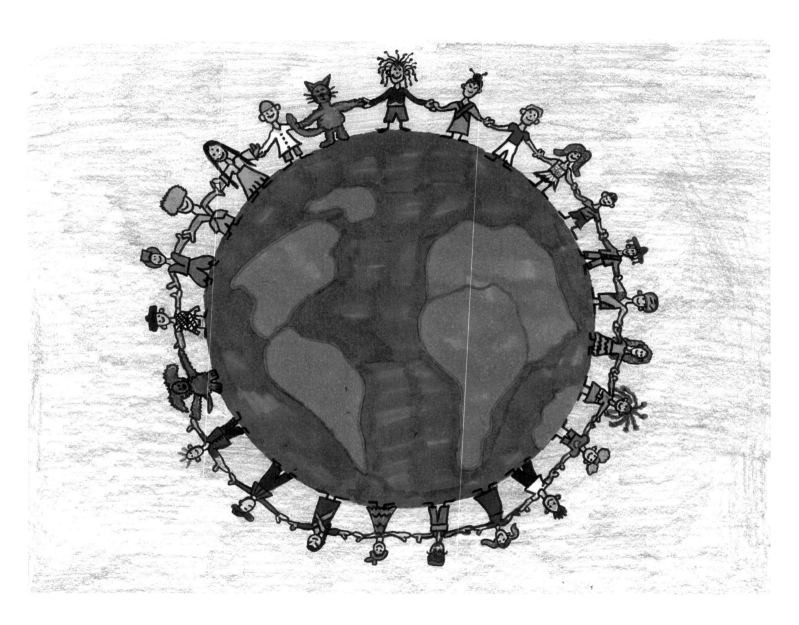

on earth

en la tierra

as it is in heaven.

como en el cielo.

Give us this day our daily bread;

Danos hoy el pan de cada día;

and forgive us our debts,

y perdona nuestras ofensas,

as we forgive our debtors;

como nosotros perdonamos a los que nos ofenden;

lead us not into temptation,

no nos dejes caer en tentación,

but deliver us from evil.

y líbranos de mal.

Amen

Amén

CPSIA information can be obtained
at www.ICGtesting.com
Printed in the USA
LVIW020826190113

316383LV00002B